This Book Belongs To:

....

Illustrated by Caroline Pedler
Retold by Gaby Goldsack

This edition published by Parragon in 2009

Parragon
Queen Street House
4 Queen Street
Bath BA1 1HE, UK

Copyright © Parragon Books Ltd 2003

ISBN 978-1-4075-8852-0
Printed in China

The Little
Fir-tree

PaRragon
Bath · New York · Singapore · Hong Kong · Cologne · Delhi · Melbourne

Deep in the forest, quite hidden from view
among the tall pines, a small fir-tree grew.
The taller trees laughed when they heard the fir moan,
"I wish I were taller, I can't wait 'til I'm grown!"
"The forest is fun," the small fir-tree was told.
"Live for the moment. Don't wish to be old."

Two winters passed, then trees were chopped down,
trimmed of their branches and taken to town.
"Where are they going?" the little tree wails.
"They're off to the ocean to hold up some sails."
"Oh, I wish I were taller," the small fir-tree sighed.
"Then I'd be a proud mast and sail far and wide."

Soon it was Christmas and men came around
to dig the tall fir-trees from the frozen ground.
"Now those trees are special," a small robin cried.
"They're decked out in baubles and taken inside."
"Oh, my what an honour," the small fir-tree said.
"Rather than sailing, I'll do that instead."

Another year passed and Christmas Eve dawned.
"The woodsmen are coming," the early bird warned.
"Oh, my, what a beauty," the old woodsman cried,
and dug up the small fir-tree, who trembled with pride.
"At last," sighed the fir-tree, as he left the warm earth.
"The time has arrived to show what I'm worth."

But when he was leaving, he didn't feel glad.
Instead he felt tearful and terribly sad.
He called to the birds, the rabbits and deer
and all of the friends that he'd grown up so near.
And with that farewell, he was carried away,
and thrown on the back of a bumpety sleigh.

Arriving at a grand house beneath the full moon,
the fir-tree was put in a magnificent room.
Decked out with tinsel, and finished with bows,
the fir-tree was splendid from his head to his toes.
The children clapped and shouted with glee,
as the fir-tree stood proudly – a tall, handsome tree.

On Christmas day, from his green boughs,
children picked presents for hours and hours.
Then there was dancing, feasting and drink.
The tree was so happy, he started to think,
"My new friends adore me and seem very kind."
He forgot to feel sad that he'd left friends behind.

And as day turned to evening, a story was told,
that dazzled the fir-tree with deeds brave and bold.
When it was over he swayed with delight,
as the room emptied with calls of goodnight.
"What joy," thought the fir-tree. "I'm glad that I came.
I can't wait 'til tomorrow for more of the same."

The proud fir-tree thought, "This is where I belong."
But when morning dawned it seemed he was wrong.
Dragged from the fine room, he was bundled away
and thrust in an old shed with no light of day.
Then out of the darkness, he heard something squeak,
he felt his twigs rustle, heard the patter of feet.

"Hello," said a white mouse. "Why are you here?
Tell us your story as we see in the New Year."
And so he told tales of his youth long ago,
of the birds, the animals and the deep, crispy snow.
As the mice gasped in wonder at all he had done,
the tree understood that the forest had been fun.

And so the tree slumbered away in the shed,
dreaming of forests and fresh air, instead,
until he was shaken awake by the noise
of children who'd come in search of their toys.
"Look it's our fir-tree," a little voice cried.
"Let's shake off the dust and plant it outside."

And from that beginning, much to his surprise,
the fir-tree grew strong and terribly wise.
Now down in the garden the big fir-tree grows,
spreading the wisdom of all that he knows.
"Youth is a blessing and nature is best.
Live for the moment, and not for the rest."